Kushka

Printed in the United States
ISBN: 978-1-935592-97-6

Written by Eli Kowalski
Illustrated by Jim McWeeney
Cover and Interior Design by Ilene Griff Design

Philadelphia, PA 19102
267-847-9018
www.sportschallengenetwork.com

Kushka Visits the Zoo

by
Eli Kowalski

illustrated by
Jim McWeeney

Today is going to be a special day. Kushka's mommy and daddy are so excited because they are taking Kushka on her very first visit to the zoo.

Kushka loves to play with her stuffed animals, and now she is going to see the real animals.

2

As Kushka and her mommy and daddy approach the zoo entrance, a special someone is waiting for them. It's Tasha, Kushka's good friend and neighbor.

Tasha waves to Kushka and says, "Hurry up Kushka, we have a very busy day today seeing all the animals."

As Kushka, Tasha and Kushka's mommy and daddy enter the zoo, they are greeted by one of the many zookeepers.

WELCOME

ENJOY YOUR DAY AT THE ZOO

BIRD HOUSE

CONGO

REPTILES

PETTING ZOO

Because the zoo is such a large place with many attractions, they ask the lady zookeeper to help them with directions. She points the four of them straight ahead toward the Swan Lake.

Kushka and Tasha are very excited, so they walk a little faster than Kushka's mommy and daddy. Kushka passes the large white swan that is swimming in the lake and she is fascinated by a beautiful bird she had never seen before. Tasha whispers to Kushka, "Don't get too close; you don't want to scare the peacock away." Then the peacock opens her feathers for all to see.

"That's a good girl, Kushka. We are going to have all day today walking around and seeing all these animals. Now let's go inside the Bird House and see some other interesting birds."

While Kushka's mommy and daddy are looking at the small bird display, Tasha and Kushka go over to look at the larger birds. They see two toucans, a bald eagle and a pelican sitting on a perch. Kushka is amazed by the size of the bald eagle's wings.

BALD EAGLE

OUCAN

As they are leaving the Bird House, they hear some strange noises. After climbing a little hill, they approach the Arctic Adventure. This is from where the noises were coming. Here they see a few penguins with happy feet, some seals playing around, a loud polar bear, and a walrus.

ARCTIC ADVENTURE

The walrus rests comfortably as the four of them walk by. "Normally these animals live in very cold weather where there is lots of snow and ice," Tasha tells Kushka.

They walk into the exhibit just past the Arctic Adventure - the Aquarium. Wow! Look how large those fish are. Most of these fish live in the ocean, but here at the zoo, they live in the aquarium. Kushka watches the fish swim past them while Tasha waves to them.

S.S. AQUARIUM

As the large shark swims past, it looks like he is smiling. Tasha remarks, "There are so many fish in this aquarium. Let me see if I know all their names. I see a jellyfish, a swordfish, a whale, a dolphin, a stingray, an eel and a sea horse. They all look like they are floating in space, but it's really water. I can stand here for hours looking at all these fish."

"That was fun watching those large mammals swim in the aquarium, but I'm getting hungry," Kushka says. Kushka starts dancing and running around in circles. She smells her favorite treat, popcorn, and gets all excited as Tasha and Kushka's mommy and daddy smile. Kushka's parents buy Kushka and Tasha a box of popcorn to share.

Kushka's mommy and daddy go sit on the bench while Tasha sees her friend Maia riding the carousel with her dog Raven. Maia waves to Tasha as she passes by. Kushka wants to jump on too, but she has to wait until the carousel stops. Tasha tells Kushka that they will go on next, as Kushka waits eagerly.

13

Around the corner from the carousel, Tasha tells Kushka to hurry. Quietly, Kushka and Tasha look at the chimpanzees and an orangutan mom cuddling her baby.

CHIMPANZEE

ORANGUTAN

On the other side of the ape
exhibit, Kushka sees a big gorilla. He is at least 100 times the size of Kushka. The gorilla
just stands there looking at Kushka, while she wags her tail. Kushka thinks this is funny.

Tasha sees the petting zoo area and wants to go pet the animals. Kushka's dad likes the petting zoo too. Here you can go inside and pet all the friendly animals.

PRIMATES

SNACK BAR

PETT

"Me too, me too," Kushka says, as she watches her daddy pet the horse. Kushka sees many children petting the animals.

16

There are so many different animals in the petting zoo.

Let's see if you can find them all.
Do you see any chickens?
Can you find the ducks?
Do you see any pigs?
Where is the rabbit?
Where is the sheep?
Where is the llama?
Do you see a deer?
Where is the goat?

NG ZOO

Then Kushka's daddy has an idea. "Let's get some food to feed the horse," he says.

Kushka jumps into her mommy's arms and watches as her mommy feeds the horse. The horse looks like he likes the treats that Kushka's mommy gives him.

Kushka keeps smiling at the horse, wondering if she is also going to get a treat.

Just past the petting zoo, Kushka and Tasha hear some music and see a clown juggling a few green balls. Tasha thinks that Kushka wants to join in the fun. She is already dancing with the clown. What do you think the monkey is going to do?

REPTILE HOUSE

After watching the clown juggle, everyone walks into the Reptile House. When they walk in, they see another zookeeper holding an iguana. Kushka is amazed by how still the iguana is while sitting in the zookeeper's hand. But, the iguana's eyes look back and forth at Kushka. Tasha asks if she could pet the iguana.

As they all walk deeper into the Reptile House, they notice a stone wall with animals behind it. "Let me see, let me see," Kushka says. Kushka wants her mommy to pick her up so she can look at some of the other reptiles.

When her mommy picks her up, she is able to see the slithering snake, a very large crocodile, a lizard, and the large shell turtle.

When they walk
out of the Reptile
House, they hear a few roars.
Kushka's daddy says, "Hurry
up, let's go see what's making
all that noise." "It's the bears,"
Kushka's mommy remarks.

"Look at the cute baby
cub sitting next to her mommy, and that
must be the papa bear over there."

BEAR COUNTRY

PANDA

Kushka turns her head to
the side and watches this big black and white panda
bear hugging the tree. Kushka asks,
"Do you think the panda bear
can climb up
the tree?"

25

The next exhibit is the Big Cat Country, where Kushka looks at the lions and tigers. Because of the protective wall, Kushka needs

to be picked up by her mommy to get a better look. She sees a black panther, an African lion, a cheetah, and a puma.

26

These animals usually look for food late at night in the jungle, but here at the zoo they are fed by the zookeepers.

The next section is the largest and most popular at the zoo. It is the African animals section. Kushka, her mommy and daddy, and Tasha hopped on the monorail to travel to this section of the zoo.

CITY ZOO

MONORAIL

The ride was very exciting because they could look out the windows and see the zoo from above. Who could miss the giraffe? He is the tallest animal at the zoo. The hippopotamus, one of the heaviest animals in the wild, plays in the water. They also see a zebra, a gazelle and some elephants wandering around.

The last stop on the zoo's monorail is the gift shop. Here Kushka meets another friend who is visiting the zoo. Her name is Sofie. Tasha looks at Sofie and tells her that Kushka created a special scavenger hunt for them and that they need to find some hidden items throughout the gift shop.

So look really carefully and see if you can find these items - an ice cream cone, popcorn, a pink hat, a soccer ball, and a pencil. Can you also find the baseball glove, a book, a magnifying glass, the duck, a dog bone, a pretzel and Bernie's face? (HINTS ARE LOCATED ON PAGE 32)

As everybody leaves the zoo, Tasha waves goodbye to Kushka. This was a wonderful day at the zoo. Kushka knows she'll be back for another visit.

It's been a very long day and Kushka cannot wait until she gets in the car so that she can close her eyes and take a nap on the ride home. What a wonderful day this was!

HIDDEN OBJECTS HINTS:
ICE CREAM CONE - in pattern of skirt; POPCORN - on gift shop sign; PINK HAT - in barrel of bounce balls; SOCCER BALL - on bottom of stuffed tiger paw; PENCIL - on clock; BASEBALL GLOVE - in hair bun of cashier; BOOK - in front of cash register; MAGNIFYING GLASS - on zoo poster; DUCK - hidden in flowers; DOG BONE - on sign post; PRETZEL - in butterfly pattern on front of counter; BERNIE'S FACE- in butterfly pattern on front of counter

Kushka was born on May 30, 2005. She is a purebred white Maltese. Her name Kushka means "cat" in Russian. She was named this because Kushka believes that she is a feline. She likes to play with many stuffed animals and takes naps on her stuffed Saint Bernard whose name is "Bernie." Kushka also likes to wear many different hats on her head. She loves the color pink and her favorite number is 177, which has special meaning to her. Over the past few years, Kushka has visited many elementary school classrooms, special needs schools, and book fairs and has appeared at outdoor festivals. Thousands of children of all ages have been entertained by her. Everyone comments on her beautiful, long, silky white hair and her cute bangs. Some have even remarked that they have seen Kushka smile at them. Kushka is a very well-behaved dog, even if she does think she is a cat.

In 2010, her first book, *Kushka, the Dog Named Cat,* was released. Kushka was introduced to all of us in this book. Kushka's other books will include *Kushka Travels the World* and *Kushka Learns Her ABC's.*

Kushka has received hundreds of emails from her fans all over the world, including Russia, Germany, Sweden, China, Italy, Spain and England, just to name a few. She even has a facebook page – Kushka the Dog Named Cat. You can friend her anytime.

If you would like to write to Kushka, please email her at Kushka@mykushka.com.

Visit Kushka's web site, www.mykushka.com, to see her schedule, download free material and learn more about her upcoming projects.